FOURTH OF JULY

by Barbara M. Joosse · Pictures by Emily Arnold McCully

Alfred A. Knopf · New York

Other books by Barbara M. Joosse

Spiders in the Fruit Cellar

The Thinking Place

This is a Borzoi Book published by Alfred A. Knopf, Inc.
Text copyright © 1985 by Barbara M. Joosse. Illustrations copyright © 1985 by Emily Arnold McCully.
All rights reserved under International and Pan-American Copyright Conventions. Published in the
United States by Alfred A. Knopf, Inc., New York, and simultaneously in Canada by Random House
of Canada Limited, Toronto. Distributed by Random House, Inc., New York.
Manufactured in the United States of America   10   9   8   7   6   5   4   3   2   1

Library of Congress Cataloging in Publication Data
Joosse, Barbara M. Fourth of July. Summary: Five-year-old Ross is often told "wait until you are six,"
but when he carries a banner to the end of a long, hot Fourth of July parade, his parents decide that
he is old enough for sparklers after all. [1. Fourth of July—Fiction] I. McCully, Emily Arnold, ill.
II. Title. PZ7.J7435Fo 1985 [E] 82-17301 ISBN 0-394-85195-1 ISBN 0-394-95195-6 (lib. bdg.)

To ANNEKE,
who sparkles like the Fourth of July,
and who always
always
tried to act six.

MY NAME IS ROSS. But my dad calls me "Rossie" and my mama calls me "honey."

I am five, which is old enough to do a lot of things if my parents would let me.

Yesterday I wanted to cross the street by myself. I said I would cross at the corner. I said I would look both ways and walk carefully. But Mama said, "Wait until you are six," and held my hand to cross.

"Wait until you are six," Dad said when I wanted a two-wheeler (that I would *not* have ridden off the sidewalk).

"Wait until you are six," Mama said when I wanted a kitten (that I promised promised *promised* to take care of).

"Wait until you are six," Dad said when I asked for poster paints (that I would *never* have used on the walls).

"When you are six," they say, "you might be old enough to be careful and to finish what you start. We'll see," they say, "when you are six."

There is one thing I am old enough to do now. March. March in the Fourth of July parade and carry a banner in front of the Grafton High School Band.

And today is the Fourth of July.

I am thinking about marching when I go to the kitchen for breakfast.

I am thinking about the gold shiny fringe on the banner when Dad
pours milk on my cereal.

I am thinking about whistles and drums and cheering when Mama
says, "You'd better stop daydreaming, honey, and eat your breakfast.
You don't want to be late for the parade."

I take a long breath. "OK," I say, and eat a bite of cereal.

"Do you know why we have a parade, Rossie?" asks Dad.
"Because it's the Fourth of July," I say.

"Right," says Dad. "And the Fourth of July is the United States' birthday."

"That is why," Mama says, "we have picnics and speeches and parades."

"And sparklers," I say.

"No sparklers," says Mama.

"Please, sparklers," I say.

"Absolutely not," says Mama.

"Why not?" I say.

"Because," says Mama, "sparklers can be dangerous. You have to be very careful with them. I don't think a five-year-old boy can be careful enough to use sparklers."

"What if I were six?" I ask, sitting up straight, trying to look tall enough to be six.

"Maybe if you were six," says Mama. "But you are only five. And sitting taller does not make you six. It is how old you act, not how old you look."

"Then," I say, "I will act six."

I go upstairs to get dressed for the parade. Without being told. I choose clothes that are red, white, and blue, the colors of the flag.

Next I clean up my room. I start putting my toys away. Puzzle pieces in the box. Records in the cases. Books on the shelf. People back in the castle.

I wonder where that king is?

In the dungeon! I'll get the queen to rescue him.
She is galloping on her horse to get the king...

...when I remember the parade. I put the rest of the toys away, and not under the bed. I put my dirty clothes in the laundry basket, and not back in my drawer. I even throw away the gum that I was hiding because I'm only allowed to chew the sugarless kind.

I save one piece in case I need it for trading or something.

My room looks like the very neat room of a six-year-old boy.
I throw away the last piece of gum.

I say goodbye to Mama and Dad.

"Don't you want us to take you to the parade?" Dad asks.

"No," I say. "I can walk by myself."

"OK, Rossie," says Dad, "but remember to hurry."

"Good luck," says Mama, waving. "We'll meet you at Millpond Park, at the end of the parade."

Then I walk to the parking lot on the corner of my block. That is the place where the parade will begin.

On the way, I pass Erdmann's Drug Store. Erdmann's has a soda fountain. Even though it is very hot, and even though I want to, I do not stop for a grape snowcone.

If I stopped, I might be late. If I stopped, I might spill snowcone on my shirt, and the colors of the flag are not red, white, blue, and purple. I am sure a six-year-old boy would not stop.

At the parking lot, the Parade Marshall hands one side of the banner to me. A big boy is carrying the other side. The drums start drumming, the horns start blowing, and the Parade Marshall blows his whistle.

We march.

I hold the banner very high and march with my knees pointing up, pointing up, like I practiced.

I pass the furniture store. I am still marching, but I am getting very hot.

I pass the gas station. I am still marching, but I am getting hot *and* tired.

Now I am hot and tired and thirsty. I think about the grape snowcone.

I pass Doyle's Dime Store. I think about the squirt guns on Doyle's counter...I think about them filled with cool water.

I pass the picture studio and I think about snowcones and squirt guns and quitting. But I keep marching because I know that a six-year-old boy would not quit.

I call to the lady with the water bottle. She gives me a drink.

We pass Stern's Grocery Store. I am so tired, my arm is practically broken from holding this banner. I am so hot I would like to run home and dunk my head in the fish tank.

I would rather get a shot, I would rather wear a tie, I would rather be too sick to go swimming than march another step in this parade.

But I keep marching marching marching. All the way to Millpond
Park. All the way…

...to the end. There are Mama and Dad.
They are waving and cheering and somebody is taking my picture.

Now we are going home. I let Dad carry me piggyback because even a six-year-old boy would do that.

On the way, we stop at Erdmann's for grape snowcones. Mine is cold and icy and delicious. It is also purple and it has dripped onto my shirt. But it doesn't matter, because the parade is over.

When I've finished, Mama hands me a napkin, and then a paper bag. Inside the bag are sparklers. Six sparklers, enough for a six-year-old boy.

Now it is the night of the Fourth of July. My sparkler is lit. I hold
it high in the air, like a birthday candle for me and the United States.
I wave it and it crackles and sparkles like fireworks.

I pretend I am directing a band with my sparkler, waving it in time to the marching music.

But I am careful. I do not drop the sparkler. I do not get it near anyone's face or clothes. I do not touch the tip when it is done burning. I am careful.

Dad lights another sparkler for me and I write my name. Ross Ross Ross in the night sky. Ross Ross Ross at the stars and the moon on the Fourth of July.

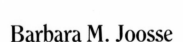

Barbara M. Joosse
has always wanted to march in a
parade. *Fourth of July* is set in
Grafton, Wisconsin, her hometown.
She now lives in Hartford, Wisconsin,
with her husband and their three children. Her previous books are *The
Thinking Place* and *Spiders in the Fruit
Cellar,* both published by Knopf.

Emily Arnold McCully
has been drawing since she was three.
The illustrator of some 100 books for
children, Ms. McCully has received
numerous citations for her graphic
work. She divides her time between
Chatham, New York, and New York
City.